MICH SKYNER

The Monkey's Fart

A BOOK OF SILLY VERSE AND NONSENSE FOR KIDS

funreads books

Illustrations by Nicola Kulesza:

Nicolajayneillustration.com

Graphic Design by Andy Kulesza Contact:

andy.kulesza@gmail.com

The book is an exploration of our English language in a way that is fun, fun, fun.

Jo Mahler Dyslexia Action

I applaud Mike's attempt to present kids - any kids, but particularly kids daunted by poetry, whatever the reasons - with the toolkit to be creative, to get writing and have fun.

Stephen Edden

author of The Word Smith's Tale
http://www.amazon.co.uk/The-Wordsmiths-Tale-Stephen-Edden/

Foreword by Charley Boorman

It's Okay
To write poet-ray
Poetry can be fun
It doesn't matter if it
Rhymes with bum
Or no rhyme at all
Ain't no crime
It's what you think
And to use words like stink
And smell, and others too
Daft to tell
But where to start
Just try the heart

Words don't have to be scary

Charley Boorman

Actor, writer, producer, Charley Boorman has acted in many films and is famous for the Long Way Round series on TV, and Road to Dakar. Charley is currently President of Dyslexia Action.

Contents

Mr Nobody

I'm a nobody
Nobody knows me
I don't know you
And you don't know me
How can I be?
If I don't know who I don't know
And who I don't know doesn't know me
What a funny fella
I must be

This is a picture of me
But nobody knows I'm here.

King Knut

Old King Knut
Sat on his tut
Eating his curds and whey
When along came a hairy Viking
And bashed him on the head
Boy did he have a headache that day

Jolly Jumping Josephit

Jolly Jumping Josephit
Jumped into a jelly pit
It's a bit smelly he thought
A smelly old jelly pit

Doggy Doos

My dog does doggy doos
Especially in the park
So, it doesn't pay to go out in the park after dark
She thinks she's given me a present
But I tell her it's not very pleasant

The Big Galoopha

The Big Galoopha went to the park to play
With the children of the day
While he was there, he saw
A stranger talking to a Teddy Bear
So, the police came and took the Teddy
Bear away

Lembit The Lion

Lembit the Lion
Crawled out of his den
And looked about to see what he ken
Let's have some fun, thought Lembit
As he started to run
Soon after a fashion
He spied a Macrashion
And thought
Now he's a good sport
I'll have him to lunch
But first I will play
So Lembit the Lion bounded hither and thither
While the Macrashion munched nonchalantly away
'If you are not going to play
I will eat you,' said Lembit
'You can't, I'm too full,' said the Macrashion
Who had had enough food for one day

Cat Pig

Cat pig is a very contented cat
That's because he is so fat
He sleeps all day
And snores all night
Lying happily on his mat
But beware of his stare
Should a cake or pie be there
For like a bat
Cat pig will fly off his mat
And all that will be left is crumbs

The Wide Mouth Frog

One day a Wide Mouth Frog
went leaping and hopping about
playing happily on a lily pond,
until he came across a giant toad
'Hello Mr. Toad,' said the Wide Mouth Frog
'I'm a Wide Mouth Frog
How do you do?'
'I'm a toad and I eat
Wide Mouth Frogs,' said Mr. Toad
To which the Wide Mouth Frog replied...

'You don't see many of those do you...
You don't see many of those...'

The Delusions of Mr. Thin

Mr.Thin was a skinny man
Who hardly ate his dinner
He didn't snack; he didn't nibble
He didn't eat between his meals
He could hardly have been thinner
But when Mr.Thin looked into the mirror
All he saw
Was a huge fridge door of a body
With a head on top
And two feet on the floor,
and arms the size of a gorilla
Poor Mr. Thin
He thought he was fat
When all the time he was as thin as a Lat
So, he went on a diet and disappeared

Jibbering Jim

Jibbering Jim was a wreck of a man
Whose nerves were all of a tremor
At the slightest sound
He would jump up and down
And quiver and quake
And shiver and shake
And become so upset
He would throw up all over his dinner

Mr. Grump

Mr. Grump had a harrumph
About nothing in particular
You see, he gets upset
Over the slightest mishap
Or to use the vernacular
He's a grumpy, wumpy, mumpy, old man

Harrumph went Mr. Grump
Kids today are not the same
There's no respect you see
Not like in my day
When we used to climb up peoples' trees
And pinch their apples
Or played postman's knock on nice folks' doors
And ran away with glee

Or pulled faces at old droopy drawers
Who lived along the way
And I remember how we used to throw stones at
Mr. Jones' shed
And he'd come out of his house shaking his fists;
with his face all red

Then there was farmer Giles' hay rick in which we
used to play
I remember setting fire to it one day
But enough said of times gone by
It's the kids today that make me angry
There's no respect you see
For my generation
The elderly

My Left Brain

(A ~~dslehic~~... a ~~dsylexic~~... a dyslexic... writing a poem)

My left brain does wot... or should that be what?
The right should do
And my right brain does the left
Is it any wonder then
That I'm somewhat bereft
When it comes to reedin, ritin and spelin
And seeing funny words and writing sed instead of said

And another thing...
Why is it we spell said said, when it   sounds like sed?
Oh! I don't ~~no, now,~~ know, and anyway Mum's just
shouted that it's time to go to ded or should that be
bed?

Is that a b or d?
I cannot tell
The writing won't stop still you see
But gimbles and bimbles all over
the page with alacrity

I think I'm in writing hell

My brain is knotted
My brow is wrinkled
My face is contorted with the effort
I write with my hand but think with my pen
My brain says rite... or is that write
But then goes left again

I look at the page
And see only space
I ~~swair~~, ~~swere~~, swear,
I could have seen a face
But I've had enough of this
writing lark
I think I'll go and play ballfoot instead

dyslexic graffiti
Kilroy ~~wos~~, was, ~~woz~~ here...

PC Knobbly Knees

Poor PC Knobbly Knees
His knees are so knobbly
It's like he has a disease
The way he hobbles along the cobbles
And wobbles up the street
With a clippity clop
And a clackity clack
You can hear him coming from a mile away
And that's a fact

Which kind a makes his job as a policeman somewhat
difficult
As the burglars have no fear
'Cos, they always know when old knobbly knees is near
But then, one day PC Knobbly Knees found an oil can
lying on the ground
That will do the trick nicely
Thought PC Knobbly Knees
And all the burglars were nicked

Polly Polynesia

Polly Polynesia was a
pernickety parrot
She was always picking at
her food
And spitting out a carrot
'Polly wants a cracker?'
'Polly wants a cracker?' they
cried
But Polly Polynesia
There really was no
pleasing her
She would always turn her
beak aside
And cackled that she didn't care
So, they stopped feeding her
And she died
Poor old Polly Polynesia

The Spider and the Macaroon

The Spider and the Macaroon
Got together for the day
And being of a merry disposition
Began to dance and sway
To the tune of a thousand crocodiles
On the road to old Bombay

They danced all night
And in the morning light pranced around till dawn
They tap danced in the busy streets
And tippy-toed on the lawn
They twirled and twirled around the countryside
And twizzled about the town
Nothing seemed to get them down

They frolicked in the rivers
And leapt across the streams

Nothing could tire them it seems
They skipped in the valleys
And danced right over the moon
Nothing it seemed could make them swoon

They wriggled and jiggled to a rapacious beat
They moved so fast you could hardly see their feet
Until one day, in the merry month of May
By the joob, joob, tree, they stopped
'I'm tired,' said the Spider
And the Macaroon swooned
Their feet it seemed were finally deadbeat
The Spider had spun its final web
And the Macaroon was cocooned in bed

The Smellyfant

(Like an elephant but much, much smellier)

A little boy goes to see his grandad and asks if he has any stories to tell. 'Aye,' says his grandad, who is from up north. 'I'll tell thee one if thou as arf a mind to lissen,' says the little boy's grandad. 'I'll tell ee a riddle.'

'How do you get a smellyfant into a fridge?'

'You can't,' said the little boy.

'Simple,' said the grandad. 'You open the fridge door and place him inside.'

'You can't, the fridge is too small,' said the small boy.

'Not if you have a fridge three metres high and three metres wide.'

'Groan.'

'How do you get two smellyfants into a fridge?'

'Give up.'

'You take the first smellyfant out and place the second one in.'

'But that's not putting two smellyfants into a fridge,' said the boy.

'Yes, it is, I didn't say they had to be in there at the same time now did I,' said the grandad.

'How do you get three smellyfants into a fridge?'

'Give up,' said the little boy.

'With great difficulty,' said the grandad.

Triple groan from the little boy.

Nosey Susan

Nosey Susan was an inquisitive girl
She couldn't keep her nose out of other
Peoples' affairs
She looked into their bedrooms
And into the cupboard under the stairs
She peered through keyholes
And earwigged through their walls
She rummaged through their garbage
Leaving out the cabbages
Of course
Nosey Susan
She just couldn't help herself
She snitched on her brother
And ratted on the cat, and on her best friend as well
And, as far as we can tell
At school she found herself to be a most unpopular girl
Then, one day, Nosey Susan spied an old well behind
her grandmother's house
Nosey Susan couldn't help herself and leaning over, she
fell into the well
Well, Well, Well
Nosey Susan is now in hell

O'Flattery the Flea

O' Flattery was a greedy flea
Not content was he
On feeding on cattle or mouldy cheese
Or crumbs left on the floor
O' Flattery would feed on everything he saw

So, he sucked on the cat's back
And dined out on the dog's dinner
He sucked up some sugar
And slurped up something gooey which was stuck on
the door

But the ultimate in heaven was when O' Flattery saw
something nasty on the floor
Oh, that will do nicely, said O' Flattery
As he sipped away with glee
But O' Flattery made a mistake
The day he spied some chocolate cake
Now alas, no more is he O' Flattery
Nothing, but a very flat and squished old flea

My Girlfriend

My girlfriend's rather big
She's twice the size of me you see
She has tattoos on her arms
And a big stud in her nose
With hair growing on her knobbly knees
All the way down to her toes
Her teeth are black
She's as ugly as a bat
Her arms are sweaty
And she swears like
Mary McClean from 5c
Who's been banned from school you see
When we go out for a walk
The other kids stare and laugh
So, my girlfriend with an almighty thump
Gives them a bump on the head
Now I can see
Why my girlfriend and I
Are so happy

The Hurgle Burgle Man

The Hurgle Burgle man is not someone or something
you want to meet
For he creeps about at night
While the rest of us are asleep
He rattles on the doorknob
And scutters on the shutters
If he is not successful
He moans to himself and mutters
And climbs up peoples' gutters
Spying a large chimney
The Hurgle Burgle man cries out with glee
'Now I can go on a burgling spree.'
But unfortunately for the Hurgle Burgle man
He's not very bright you see
For weighing in at fifteen stone
His girth was too tight for the chimney
And he got stuck
Now the Hurgle Burgle man
He isn't 'urgling no more
But has only porridge for company

How do you Eat an Elephant?

Q: How do you eat an elephant?

A: Very slowly.

The Walrus and the Carpenter Revisited

(A tribute to Lewis Carroll)

'Mr. Walrus,' said the Carpenter
'Let's go for a little lunch
There's a nice spot near the jungle
If it won't trifle you too much.'

'Certainly,' said the Walrus
'That's a splendid idea
But aren't you frightened of the elephants?
They might trample us if they are near?'

'Not if we muffle our feet,' said the
Carpenter
'For then the elephants will not hear.'
So, they set off for the jungle
With a staple diet of bread and cheese
And a bottle of good cheer

They tramped and tramped for many a mile
Until they found the perfect spot
'This will do nicely,' said the Walrus
And they sat down in a jot

'Oh, dear me,' said the Walrus
'I do feel quite queer
The ground appears to be moving
And, at a funny angle I fear.'

The ground indeed, began to wobble
And they both took a tumble
As up stood an irate elephant
Who had been slumbering in the grass

Cried the Walrus
'You battle with the front end
And I'll juggle with the back.'
But the struggle was uneven
And the outcome was soon clear

For with a mighty roar and shake of its trunk
Walrus and Carpenter far and wide, were flung
And, the elephant sat down to the sumptuous feast
Which they unwittingly did provide

Adapted from Lewis Carroll
The Walrus and the Carpenter.

Be Careful what you Wolf For

(A Short Story)

Wolf was hungry.

Actually, this was an understatement. Wolf was positively ravenous. It had been days since his last meal. All you can eat, guaranteed, said the contract. So, it was with great excitement and a somewhat indecent amount of salivation, that Wolf made his way into the woods.

Wolf padded through the bushes, leaving behind an anticipatory trail of drool, as he went. At precisely two o'clock, Little Red Riding Hood would be passing this way to see her infernal granny. Wolf crept from tree to tree, making sure he would not be seen, seeking the best spot from which he could leap out and attack his prey.

Wolf waited and waited. Two o'clock came and went, two-thirty, three and still no sign of his quarry.

Then he heard it, faintly at first, then louder and louder. Someone or something was approaching, or rather, he felt it. The ground trembled and shook. Birds flew off to their nests. The trees and shrubs were being swept aside to the accompaniment of loud crashing sounds.

'Hang on a minute, that's not right,' said Wolf, as he checked his contract.

Little Red Riding Hood would come skipping gaily through the woods, with a light gait, holding a bunch of goodies.

Wolf folded the contract back up again. The sounds grew louder.

'Sounds more like a herd of elephants with attitude,' said Wolf to himself.

Wolf waited nervously. The noise was now deafening. At last, the bushes in front of Wolf were swept aside. To reveal... a giant in a red hoodie.

An enormous fat red blob of a creature stood before Wolf. Wolf couldn't see the face because of the hood. Startled, Wolf took an involuntary step backwards. Could this be the Little Red Riding Hood that he had been led to expect? Obviously, there had been a few changes since they had last met. A few too many visits to the cake shop, being one.

'Er, are you by any chance Little Red Riding Hood?' asked Wolf.

'Yes I am. Who else were you expecting in a red hood, Florence Nightingale?'

Well... Wolf stared at the beast before him, taking in the fullness of her size. Bit of a bonus I suppose, more for me to eat.

But something was troubling Wolf. He could have sworn that somewhere, the script required him to dress up as Little Red Riding Hood's granny.

'Perhaps if I can see your lovely face, er... little girl.' Well, he might as well try to stick to the script.

Little Red Riding Hoodie, slowly drew back the large red hood.

Wolf gasped and shuddered, he took more involuntary steps backwards, as he tried to compose himself. Before him stood a creature which, in all his years as a professional fairy tale artist, he had never encountered the likes of before. Such were the creature's dimensions, it made Jack and the Beanstalk look mere amateurs by comparison.

'My, what big ears you have,' said Wolf, mesmerized by the jug-like flesh monsters which hung down either side of the creature's head. The elephantine ears were bedecked with jewels which enhanced the grotesqueness rather than reduced the hideousness. Wolf was beside himself.

'Er... my, what big...' Wolf took in the forest-like eyebrows which met together like a copse in the middle of the forehead. And he could hardly fail to miss the cauliflower nose, resplendent with black, hairy wart. Wolf was lost for words.

Little Red Riding Hoodie smiled. Well, we think of it as a smile, more a grimace from the jaws of hell. But at least Wolf was on familiar territory. Back to the script.

'My, what big teeth...' Wolf paused as six enormous razor-sharp fangs emerged... 'you have,' gulped Wolf.

'Hang on, this isn't the script at all.' Wolf took out the paper in his pocket, quickly glancing at the script. 'She should be asking me that... this isn't right?'

The giant Red Riding Hoodie disrobed. The hood fluttered to the ground to reveal the creature in all its glory.

Did I say glory?

Wolf stood trancelike at the giant spectacle of the creature standing before him. He took in the rolls of blubbery flesh; the jungle of hair from the armpits; the eruptions emerging from the primeval swamp of the nostrils.

Wolf swallowed hard as he noted the glistening beads of sweat gleaming all over the moonscape of the flesh mountain, encased in a bright lemon leotard.

This, decided wolf, was a project too much even for him to handle.

'Er, I've just remembered an urgent appointment, must dash,' said wolf, as he started to ease backwards.

'Oi!' said the giant, formerly of the red hoodie, 'where do you think you're going? You're supposed to eat me. It's in the contract.'

'Stuff the contract,' said Wolf, as he back-pedalled, running through the undergrowth. 'Come back 'ere or I'll set my granny on you.'

Wolf didn't even begin to imagine what the creature's granny was like. He didn't want to go there. He simply kept on running.

As Wolf ran, he thought about the day's events.

'Wasn't like this when I worked for Hans flipping Christian Andersen.'

'Oh, for the good old days.'

Wolf ran and ran until his chest was fit to burst. He stopped, gasping for breath. Wolf looked up. In front of him was a gingerbread house. 'Oh, goody,' said Wolf. 'Food at last.' Wolf ran in. The cottage was empty and so was the kitchen. Wolf turned to leave. He heard a noise. Wolf tip-toed into the bedroom.

Someone or something was lying in the bed, covered by a large blanket. Whatever it was, it was enormous. Even bigger that the encounter he had had earlier, if that was possible. Gingerly, Wolf drew back the cover to reveal... Little Red Riding Hood's Granny.

Wolf stood back dumbstruck. After a few seconds, he found his voice.

'Granny!' said Wolf, 'my, what big...'

They were the last words he uttered.

Maurice the Mongoose

Maurice the Mongoose was a slippery critter
When it came to baiting snakes; there was none fitter
If Maurice spied a slithery serpent, sliding by
He would natter and twitter and go up on all haunches
The snake equally fearless would reply
By giving Maurice the evil eye
And mesmerizing him with a look
Would suddenly strike out with its tongue
And from its tail; a hefty left hook
But the snake would recoil with horror
As Maurice deftly stepped aside
'You have to be quicker than that to catch me old
chum.'
And bit old snaky on the bum

The Old Man and the Wood Turner

One day, a little girl went to see her grandmother. 'Oh, do tell me a story granny,' said the little girl, as she sat on her grandma's knee. So, the grandmother told the little girl the tale of the old man and the wood turner.

The story was all about how an old man would go out into the wood every day to find chopping wood but, no matter how often he went, he simply couldn't find any wood. He had no wood to light the fire with and then, one day when he was in the wood, he came across a neatly stacked pile of logs, already chopped up for the fire.

So, he brought the wood home and the next day, he went out looking for more wood, and sure enough, there was another pile of wood all chopped up and ready to go. Then he took the wood home and used it for firewood and all in the house were happy. Except the wood turner; who was scratching his head wondering what had happened to his pile of wood.

Then, while he watched, the wood turner saw the old man taking his wood and asked him what he thought he was doing with it.

The old man told the wood turner that he needed the wood for his fire, as his family was freezing with the cold. The wood turner felt sorry for the old man's family and took pity on the old man's plight.

'Tell you what,' he said. 'If you give me a hand with turning this wood, I'll let you have some for your family.'

'That's most generous of you for sure,' said the old man.

So, the old man helped the wood turner to turn his wood, which ensured that he had enough wood to keep his family warm.

And the moral of this story is, children, that whenever you find yourself in need of someone's help, remember...

One wood turner deserves another.

Terry the Tarantula

Terry the tarantula had a spindly body and eight
skinny, hairy legs
Which intrigued the old fly who had only six
'Why do you need all those legs?' asked the fly

'Well,' said Terry, savouring his reply
'Two are for dancing and twinkling my toes
Two are for eating and picking my nose
Two are for walking and making my way
Two are for capturing and clutching my prey.'

And without another sound
Terry the tarantula grasped the old fly
within his grip and ate him.
'Yum! Yum!'

My Poor Old Bum

My bottom's sore
It's all red and blotchy you see
On account of Marvin my old adversary
We are always daring the other to see how outrageous
we can be
I challenge him to jump off an old scaffolding plank
And he challenges me to skateboard off Big Bertha
Which is a steep cliff near where we live
Then one day, Marvin says 'I challenge you to do the
unthinkable and skateboard while holding on to a
passing car.'
Well, there's nothing like a good challenge, is there?
So, off I go without a care
And sure enough
Mr. Jones of number thirty-three
Comes trundling by in his Vauxhall Verity
So, I hitch a lift and whoosh, I'm off
Flying along the street at death defying speed
Well, all was going great, until Mr. Jones turned left
as we were going down Scraptoft Hill
And I went flying over Mrs. Murtle's big white gate
On and on I flew, up, up, into the air
Until gravity took hold and I found myself crashing
through the roof of Mrs. Murtle's greenhouse
Boy, was she cross

But this was nothing compared to my Dad when he found out
Which is why I can't sit down on my bum, see
Funny really, 'cos Dad said I was grounded
But all I can do is stand up

PS. Don't do this at home kids

Brujita the Witch

Brujita was a silly old witch
She was always flying backwards
On her broomstick
Without a stitch of clothes on
Except her witch's hat of course
She never went anywhere without that
And as for her black cat, Morbidia
She never knew whether she was going to be fed
Or, turned into a rat instead
But Brujita's worst mistake
Was when she made a witches' brew instead of stew
for her Sunday lunch
Brujita flew off into the air
Growing fatter and fatter
Until with an almighty bang
She exploded all over the local fair
And, it rained cats and frogs and puppy dogs for a
whole year

Horace the Hippo

Horace the Hippo was a happy chappy
He would frolic and flipper
Up and down, over and under
In his favourite river

All day and all-night Horace would wallow in his
hollow
Without a care in the world
No sorrowful hippo he...
Horace was at his best
Having a laugh in his mud bath

Then one day a tsetse fly came whizzing by
And spotting Horace's back
Thought 'that will do nicely,
For a spot of rest and respite
And a nice cup of tea'

The fly, landing on Horace's back
Began to suck away merrily
On Horace's rear end
At first, Horace tried to ignore the fly
But flicking its tail failed miserably

And when Horace could bear it no longer
Took off downstream in mid itch
With his legs bucking to and fro
Until he fell into a ditch

Poor old Horace, he was in a right old mess
Until, spying some prickly brambles
Plunged straight in... And... Bliss

Then Horace heard a plaintive cry
'It's all right for you mate,' said the fly
'You've gone and made me spill me tea
Now I'm in a right old two and eight' (state)

My Bionic Granny

My Great Grandma's bionic
She's superhuman see
She has batteries for ears
And false teeth she keeps in a jar
The lenses in her glasses are so thick
That she can't see very far
Her hips are made of plastic
And she has a pacemaker for a heart

Most of the time she does puzzles
And she always likes to bake
Then she falls asleep
But say the word tea
And she comes alive like electricity

She wears an old shawl
And slippers on her feet
And rocks back and forth in an old arm chair
She giggles and chuckles
She doesn't seem to have a care in the world
As she strokes her old cat Cuddles

When I come to visit
She always has a treat
Of cream buns and lemonade
As much as I can eat

But best of all
Is when my Great Grandma
Gets out her broom
And flies off around the room
Twirling in her pantaloons

Mr. Mushroom

There isn't much room inside a mushroom
So why do they call them mushrooms?
Mushrooms come in all shapes and sizes
Some are tall, and some very small
Some are fat and some very thin
And some look like old Chinese Mandarins

Olly Gaitor

Olly Gaitor was not a happy croc
He was feeling down in the dumps
The problem you see was he had no chums
To play, to wallow, to talk about the day
Every time Olly went for a stroll
All the other creatures would run away
Which made poor Olly very droll
He just wanted to have a friend
To have a natter and jaw-jaw
But that was the problem
They would take one look at Olly's jaws
And that would be the last thing of
Olly they ever saw

The Madness of Mike Mcgoo

There once was a madman called Mike McGoo
Who was always getting into a bit of a stew
He thought he was an owl
And if you cried foul
He would fly off into the air and shout
Twit-twoo, Twit-twoo

There once was a madman called Mike McGoo
Who was always getting into a bit of a stew
He was so poor
He had no front door
So, he went out via the loo

There once was a madman called Mike McGoo
Who was always getting into a bit of a stew
He would upset his neighbour
With his odd behaviour
By playing all night on his kazoo

The Song of King Nungler

All hail King Nungler – the none too clever
So strong so fearless
A mighty warrior he
But when his enemies charge
He always flees

He's King Nungler – the none too clever
Great and noble
Fearsome and bold
Pity that he is so old

He's King Nungler – the none too clever
With his mighty girth
He presents a magnificent sight
But he's so fat
That when he mounts his horse
It always falls flat

He's King Nungler – the none too clever
Big and bold
And round in the belly
He never washes
And is rather smelly

He's King Nungler – the none too clever
His nose is long
He has a terrible tongue

He sucks his thumb
He's rather big in the bum
He's King Nungler – the none too clever

His eyes are furtive
His mouth is thin
His chin wobbles like jelly
And he has a lopsided grin

He's King Nungler – the none too clever
His clothes are shabby
He's rather flabby
His hair is so greasy
He makes you feel queasy

He's King Nungler – the none too clever

Birthday Party

'Don't trifle with him,' said the fairy cake
'Eat me instead
 You'll never get a better bake
'I disagree,' said the jelly
'Just add some ice cream
 It's the best thing for your belly.'
'Have a heart,' said the custard tart
'With lashings of cream, what more could you want?'
'You can't go wrong,' said the pink blancmange
'If you eat me.'
 But the birthday boy couldn't decide between
 jelly, tart and cake
 So, he ate the lot
 And got bellyache

Mr. Anxious

Mr. Anxious was always worrying
He worried about unemployment
He worried about the poor
He worried about his lumbago
And the slobs that lived next door
He worried about his loose change
It never did quite make ends meet
He worried about his food and what
was good enough to eat
He even worried about being worried
And, while he was worrying about the state of his
health
He died (He forgot to worry about that)

I Want

Said one boy to another
'I want a Nintendo Wii, then I'll be happy.'
'I want a BMX bike,' said the other,
'then I'll be alright.'
'I want a Barbie doll to add to my collection,' said the
 girl with the little curl
'I want a Game Station,' said the boy who already had
 every type of toy
'I want a puppy and doll to put in my pram,' said the
 girl whose name was Sam
'Just like my Mam.'
'I want a pony and I'll call it Tony,' said the young-un
 who stamped her feet in a tantrum
'I want a Dad, to tuck me up in bed,' said the boy whose
 Dad was dead

MacTavish the Scot

MacTavish the Scot is tall, grand and lofty
But really, he's just a big softy
He twirls aboot in his kiltie
It didn't matter that he walks with a liltie

He'd rush aboot down the glen
And toss the caber back up again

A strong man through and through
From drinking copious amounts of Irn Bru
And eating porridge, haggis and black pudding
And Mrs MacTavish, who kept on nagging
MacTavish to eat his stew, too

But best of all, MacTavish liked to play his bagpipes
And would dress up all posh with braid and sporran
But foolhardy is he who would dare
To try and lift the mackiltie and discover the secrets of
MacTavish's underwear

Little Mouse Around the House

There once was a little mouse
Who lived under the floor in our house
At night when all was quiet
Mouse would come out and forage for
titbits to supplement his diet
Spying some cereal boxes mouse would
nibble a hole in the base
Leaving on the floor, a tell-tale, trace
Then, one night, mouse got a fright
For leaving his lair
He was met with a stare
From the cat that lived next door
Now, mouse in the house, is no more

Flossie the Flamingo

Was an elegant fowl
She had bright pink cheeks
All the way to her jowls
When she plumped up her chest
To an elegant behest
Her fur was more duck down than feather

On her stork-like legs
She would preen her head
And dip her duck-bill
Along the lake bed
Looking for tasty treats
Of a larva or two

But when Flossie tries to fly
Her elegance dies
She looks to all intents and purposes
Like a demented duck
With an elephant's backside

Sunrise

The Sun rises in the morning
And, in the evening, it goes to bed
I wonder where it puts its head.

Mr. Blob

Mr. Blob was a bit of a slob
Who never could be tidy
He left his socks on the floor and his ties in meat pies
Which he ate every other Friday

Mr. Blob was a bit of a slob
Who ate until he was fit to burst
He dined on lion and whale
And even worse, would belch and tell fishmongers'
tales

Mr. Blob was a bit of a slob
Who would dribble all over his dinner
He would slobber and drool
And, as a rule, would wipe his mouth
With the back of the cat
And keep mince pies
Underneath his top hat

The U Rang U Tang

There once was an Orang-utan
Who loved to dine out
On strawberry and lemon meringue
And eat cheese sandwiches with raspberry jam
His fur was matted and bright orange
And sported a permanent suntan
From eating too many carrots
And was always being told off by his Nan
He would amble about without a care in the world
And would breeze through the trees
On a giant trapeze
And make a monkey out of people
Who would try to put him in a zoo
Then again, wouldn't you?
He would spit in their faces
And sit on their hands
And drag his knuckles all the way
Up to his chest
And bang very loudly on his string vest

The Big Twit

The Big Twit
Was a bit of a nit
He could never do anything proper
No matter how hard he tried to concentrate
He would always come a cropper

One day the Big Twit
Saw an old lady
Standing by the side of the road
Being a good scout and, not a lout
The Big Twit helped the old lady to cross
Instead of a thank you and a sweet smile
The old lady went bright red and cried
'I've just crossed that road, you big twit.'
And hit him with her walking stick

Undaunted, the Big Twit went on his way
And spying some children at play
Asked if he could join in
Picking up their ball
The Big Twit dribbled and twirled
Heading the ball with his big bonce
He hit the ball right over the fence

Not waiting to be thanked
The Big Twit went on his way
Then he spied a little girl crying
'Why are you crying little girl?'
The little girl explained that
She had lost her pet hamster called Wuffles
'I'll help you find him,' said the Big Twit

So, the Big Twit bounded hither and thither
In search of Wuffles the hamster
Suddenly he spied
Munching on some dandelions
A hamster answering to Wuffles' description

'Oh, gee,' said the Big Twit, scooping up Wuffles
'The little girl is going to be so happy.'
The Big Twit took Wuffles back to the little girl
'There, little girl, your hamster,' said the
Big Twit, placing Wuffles on the ground
'Oh, thank you,' said the little girl with glee

Just then, an alley cat
Never one to miss an opportunity for a quick snack
Bounded down and in one quick snatch
Ran off with Wuffles in its jaws
'You twit,' shouted the little girl
The Big Twit didn't know what to say
So, he bid the little girl good day

The Big Twit
Was a bit of a nit
He could never do anything proper
No matter how hard he tried to concentrate
He would always come a cropper

What Will I Be When I Grow Up Daddy?

What will I be when I grow up daddy?
Will I be famous, successful and rich?
Will I have a fast car and a big house?
Will I have a castle with a moat and a ditch?
Will I have holidays and travel afar?
Will I be an astronaut and fly to Mars?
Will I be handsome and strong like Brad Pitt?
Will I have girls swooning at my feet?
Will I be a great man and change the world?
Oh, what will I be when I grow up daddy?

If you have your health, my son, you will be rich
If you turn the other cheek, you will be strong
If you think of others, others will think good things of
 you
If you show kindness, kindness will be shown to you
If you help others, you will be helped
If you follow your conscience, you will know right from
 wrong
If you are honest and truthful, you will know not to lie
If you do all these things, you will be a great man

Then the world will be a better place
And you will truly be my son

Fire at Will

'Why do they always pick on me?

What have I done wrong?'

The Legart

The Legart is a funny looking creature
Just one eye, one leg and a giant beak its only
distinguishing features
It hops about all day
Looking for seaweed and
bits of hay
It stands for hours on one
leg
Well, it hasn't really any
choice
Stock still
Then, should anyone
unsuspecting pass by
It will lift its beak and
chortle
'Legart! Legart! Legart!'
And with a malevolent
twinkle in its eye
It will fly-hop over its
victim
Shouting 'Goodbye.'
Yes, the Legart is a funny
creature
And at night when the day
is done
The Legart will stand on its
head
And sleep upside down on its
bed

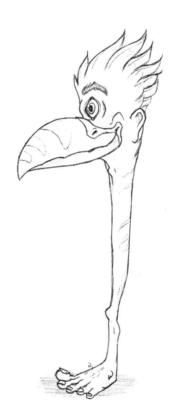

The Monkey's Fart

There was an old monkey
His fur all tatty and matted
Who lived all alone on a hill
On account of his unsociable behaviour

You see, he liked to eat the fruit of the Boff Boff tree
He would breakfast in the morning
And nibble all day
And in the evening would dine till
first light

Now as you can guess
Eating all this fruit to excess
Had some unfortunate effects
Monkey would parp in the morning
And boff during the day

He would eugh-whiff at passers-by
And thirrrp while he played
All the other creatures gave monkey a wide berth
'Such a foul-smelling creature,'
They cried

Then one day Monkey ate
Far more than his fill
He grew and grew until he was fit to burst, then
With, a mighty bang, he exploded
And bits of old monkey
Farted all over the hill

The Grongle

You'd better beware
For nobody knows
When the Grongle is there
He moves unawares
Without a care

And if he fixes you with his stare...
Oh, yes, you'd better beware
When the Grongle is there

With his long skinny neck
Bulging eyes
His lopsided smile
And pelican thighs
The Grongle is certainly
A queer looking fish

But make no mistake
For the Grongle is full of hate
If riled, his fury knows no bounds
His mercy is merciless
His revenge, exacting

So, keep on your toes
Don't blow your nose
(He doesn't like that)

And who knows
He might just let you live

And if he fixes you with his stare...
Oh, yes, you'd better beware
If the Grongle is there

The Bully

With furtive eyes
Snake-like gait
The Bully creature
Plies its trait

With troglodyte head
And sloping arms
It lopes along
Always on the alert
Waiting to select
Its next victim

'Gimme your money.'
'Gimme your phone.'
'Gimme your ice cream.'
'Or I'll never leave you alone.'

Its eyes swivel and stare
This way and that
Always on the look out
Never relax

The bully is merciless
It doesn't care
Who it hurts
No conscience there

But wait
Don't feel hate
For the bully is a pathetic weak creature
To be pitied
For the bully has no friends
No one to care
No one to love it
Who'd be a bully?
Not you!

The ACME Writing Poetry Kit

How to create your own poems with a little help from
Monkey

Monkey says: writing poetry can be fun and easy when
you know how but, like anything, there are a few rules to follow.
Let's have a look at this nonsense poem about a teacher:

Mr. McCRIEF'S TEETH

My teacher, Mr. McCrief
Has horrible, lopsided teeth
And two enormous fangs
Like an Orang-utan's
He has bug eyes which are really big
And a pug nose, just like a pig
His chin wobbles like jelly
(It matches his belly)
His ears are somewhat floppy
And his expression's a bit soppy
With such hideous, ugly features
Our teacher's a rather pathetic creature

What do you notice?
Yes, that's right, the ends of the lines rhyme.

This is called **Rhyming Couplets.**
This is the method you are probably most familiar with.

Now you try... Look at the list at the back of this section
and select a couple of pairs.
I've chosen bun, fun, head and bed.
Now let's see what we can do.

I like to eat a nice big **bun**
'Cos, I find them so much **fun**
I keep them hidden under my **head**
And eat them while I'm in my **bed**

I know it's a bit icky to keep buns under your head, but this is nonsense poetry after all.
Now you have a go...
How did you get on?
Brilliant, I expect.
Let's try again.
This time I've chosen frog, bog, choke, and croak.

I know a little **frog**
Who lives in a smelly old **bog**
And each time he tries to **croak**
The foul air starts to make him **choke**

Have another try... How did you do? Better I expect. Like anything, the more you practice, the better you become. When I write poetry, I usually just have an idea and let my pen do the work and see where it takes me. Then I work on the result. After all, to make your work shine, you need to add a little polish, and a little time.

Monkey's telling me that it's time to look at another method. This one is called the **Alternative Rhyming Couplet.** It's similar to the Rhyming Couplet method, but this time, the rhyme is on every other line.
Let's have a look at an example:

Harry was an unhappy **frog**
For every time he tried to **croak**
In the horrible, perfumed **bog**
The smell would make him **choke**

Mm, it's not brilliant, but at least it illustrates the technique. Now it's your turn. How did you do? Remember, keep it simple and keep it fun. Let your pen flow. You never know where you might go.

'What about the E**nvelope**?'
'I was just coming to that Monkey.' Let's have another look at the Frog poem:

Harry was an unhappy **frog**
And every time he tried to **croak**
The fumes would start to make him **choke**
Not much fun living in a smelly old **bog**

This time the rhyme in the middle is wrapped around by the rhyme on the outside. This is called the **Envelope method**. While we're playing around with rhyme, it's worth mentioning another technique called **Internal Rhyme**. This time the rhyme is found within the same line. Take a look at the following:

Have a **heart** said the custard **tart**
Here the rhyme is formed by heart and tart, in the same line. And again, from Mr. Slob:
And his **tie**s in meat **pies**

Can you see how the rhyme is formed by ties and pies?
'I think they get it. You haven't mentioned **Repetition** and **Alliteration**.'
'Haven't I Monkey?'

Right, well **Alliteration** is when you use similar
sounding words which often have the same first letter.

Poly Polynesia was a **p**ernickety **p**arrot
She was always **p**icking at her food
And spitting out a carrot

The rhyme is formed by repeating the first letter, in
this case P. The rhyme is completed by rhyming parrot
with carrot. This is one of my favourite methods.
You can have a lot of fun with it. Repetition can also be
very powerful. Repeating the first line can make for a
forceful impact.

Will I be famous, successful and rich?
Will I have a fast car and a big house?
Will I have a castle with a moat and a ditch?
Will I have holidays and travel afar?

You can then mirror the image using another
repetition:

If you have your health, my son, you will be rich
If you turn the other cheek, you will be strong
If you think of others, others will think good things of you
If you show kindness, kindness will be shown to you

Acrostics

(sounds like across sticks)

Acrostics are a type of verse whose first letters spell out a name, word or phrase.

Beautiful sunsets
Over the hill
Green, green, grass
Everyone enjoys
Year after Year

Mm, the acrostic doesn't quite go with the image of the poem. Here are some more…

Bug
Ugly
Lying
Little
Yob

Now don't do that
And put that down
Unlock that door
Give me that
Have you not learnt?
Told you before
You're horrible

You can have a lot of fun with acrostics just play around see what you come up with.

'I've got one, I've got one!'
'All right Monkey, go ahead.'

Poncey
Over the top
Egotistical
Twit

'Oh, thank you.'
'You're welcome.'
'Good thing I don't know what egotistical means.'
'Big head!'
'Pardon?'
'That's what it means.'
'I think it's time we moved on.'

Emotions

One of the interesting ways of writing poems is to write
about your emotions: - how do you feel - happy, sad, thoughtful or
bad, mad, or just plain angry. Imagery is a nice way of showing
emotions: balloons, bubbles and feathers are popular images for
when you are feeling happy.

I fly around without a sound
Dancing freely in the air
There's nothing to weigh me down
I drift by without a care

Or what about anger:

Agh!
Nasty
Growl
Rage
Yell

Or sadness:

My eyes are sad
I feel really bad
It wasn't my fault you see
I was only feeding the birds
How was I to know?
The cat next door
Had the same idea as me

Limericks

The limerick made famous by Edward Lear has a
special format. It follows the pattern: AABBA where the
first, and second line, rhymes with each other. Line
three and four rhyme together and the fifth line
repeats the first or rhymes with it.

A limerick is always good fun
Like eating a sticky cream bun
A great way to start
Is to eat a big tart
Then belch and fart in the sun

'You had to lower the tone, didn't you?'
'Sorry, Monkey.'

There once was a Pickannoo
Who didn't know what to do
He would dither and thither
And thither and dither
A most confused Pickannoo

There once was a kitten called Cutie
Who thought she was rather a beauty
But if you ruffled her fur
She would give out a grrr
The not so cute beauty called Cutie

There once was a lady called Jenny
Who needed to spend a penny
But a penny she had not
To put in the slot
The cross-legged lady called Jenny

There once was a bug called Dug
Who was lonely for want of a hug
So, he looked for a mate

With eight legs and long gait
Now Dug is as snug as a bug in a rug

There once was a lady from Ealing
Who got stuck on a very high ceiling
The ceiling went crack
She fell on her back
The very flat lady of Ealing

There once was a lion called Leo
Who everyone thought was a hero
But if you said boo
He would curl up in two
The cowardly lion called Leo

'Er, pardon me for saying so.'
'What is it Monkey?'
'Well, it's that last limerick; it doesn't quite
work, does it?'
'What do you mean?'
'Well, Leo doesn't rhyme with hero.'
'They both end with an O.'
'Yes, but Hero isn't quite the same sound as Leo.'
'Isn't it?'
'No.'
'It depends on how you say it.'
'Oh, I give up.'

Children are brilliant at writing limericks, so do have a
go. In my opinion, their limericks are often better than
adults'.

'They are definitely better than yours.'
'Thanks Monkey.'
(To see brill limericks by other kids, go to:
www.brownielocks.com)

Cinquain

Cinquain (which means five) is a poem or stanza comprised of five lines, with three different patterns:

ABABB, ABAAB, ABCAB,

This gives you plenty of choice and flexibility.

Line 1 One word, title or noun
(person, place or thing)

Line 2 Two adjectives describing the thing

Line 3 Three ing, participles (words that tell you what your noun does)

Line 4 A phrase or sentence about the noun

Line 5 Another word for your noun

Shark
Killer, vicious
Basking, swimming, eating
Der de, der de, der de, der de, der de
(read very fast)
Jaws

As you can see, I'm rubbish. Cinquains are an excellent way for younger children to start writing poetry.

My little brother
Horrible, smelly
Fibbing, blaming, cheating
Phor! What you got there then?
Love you, Bruv

Dog
Faithful, companion
Sniffing, fetching, chasing
Man's best friend; burier of bones
Puppy dog

Free Verse and Prose

'Tell them about Free Verse and Prose.'
'Ah, yes, thank you, Monkey.'

Free verse is very popular these days as a form of writing expression. As it doesn't involve formal rhyme, anything goes. Even so, it must have structure and have a certain rhythm or beat, if it is to work.

Look at this extract from Mr Blob:

Mr Blob was a bit of a **slob**
Who would dribble all over his dinner
He would slobber and **drool**
And, as a **rule**, would wipe his mouth
With the back of the **cat**
And keep mince pies
Underneath his top **hat**

Mm, it's not quite free verse as there is quite a bit of internal and some end rhymes.
But look at this extract from The Bully:

For the bully is a pathetic weak creature
To be pitied
For the bully has no friends
No one to care
No one to love it
Who'd be a bully?
Not you!

Apart from a little bit of repetition, this is pretty much free verse. So, my style is I suppose what you call prose poems.
'Is there much more of this? I want to start writing some poems.'
'Sorry, Monkey, almost finished, just one or two more

things to mention.'

Firstly, let's have a look at something I call
Rhyming Beats. (The technical name is Iambic Pentameter
– where penta, means five.)

De Dum, De Dum, De Dum, De Dum, De Dum,
Do you notice a pattern? Let's put in some words.

When **Mon**key **sings,** he **makes** a **dread**ful **noise**
Can you see that the rhyme is on the second syllable on each pair
of words or word? There are five stresses or beats in the line.
Now let's add another line:

And **all** the **crea**tures **cover** up **their** ears

This is called a meter with a five-beat rhythm or five feet.
Now have a look at another poem or stanza:

De Dum, de Dum, de Dum, de Dum
The **Mon**key **has** a **tale** to **tell**
Ad**ven**tures **far**, ad**ven**tures **near**
And, **if** you **lis**ten **long** e**nough**
You'll **get** a **flea** in**side** your **ear**

'Oh, very funny.'
'Sorry Monkey, couldn't help myself.'

What do you notice? That's right; there are four beats to the
line. This is the most common form of beats or stresses
used in poetry.

'I think it's time we started to write some poems.'
'I agree.'

In the following pages, I've put together some lists of words
which rhyme or go well together. You can also start
creating some lists of your own. So now it's over to you.

'Thank goodness for that.'
'Cheeky.'

Poetry is a way of expressing your feelings and emotions. My poems tend to be a mixture of methods: rhyme rhythm, repetition, free verse and prose, sometimes, with internal rhythms and beats. You now have the basic tools to write your own nonsense poems. Have fun and remember, if it sounds right, it probably is.

Word List

A few wow words and phrases just to get you started:

grubby grubs
ugly mugs
ugly bugs
squelchy belchy
smelly belly
horrid squalid
 crunchy crusts
 slurpy burps
 crumbly bumbly
crunchy munchy
wiggling worms – make you squirm.
wriggly squiggly

Now try adding some of your own.
Here are some more simple lists of rhyming words:
As you can see, it doesn't take long to make up lists of
rhyming words. Now have a go and see how many lists
you can make. You'll soon have hundreds to choose from.

fun	head	moan	teacher	Bag	sag
bun	Bed	groan	creature	Sag	snag
run	fled	flown	feature	hag	stag
sun		sown	preacher	brag	mag
one	dread	thrown	still	flag	gag
ton	bled	drone	till	rag	bug
drop	red	belt	spill	crag	rug
prop	said	pelt	thrill	drag	slug
prod	croak	lot	will	elf	mug
pod	choke	hot	feel	self	hug
trod	bog	snot	steal	bold	gut
clod	frog	splat	heel	cold	rut
pod	mob	hat	kick	told	hut
nod	rob	fat	sick	mould	nut
mask	sob	cat	clock	old	shot
bask	snob	stink	frock	hold	got
frisk	dung	pink		duck	fish
risk	rung	kitten		suck	wish
	hung	mitten		flash	
	flung			smash	

*Further Reading:

Spike Milligan's Silly Verse for Kids 1959, 1963, (Puffin Books) – Poems to look for: The Ning Nang Nong, Rain, In the Land of the Bumbley Boo, The ABC.

Quentin Blake: The Puffin Book of Nonsense Verse, 1996 – Poems to look for Jabberwocky, Walrus and the Carpenter, by Lewis Carroll. The Jumblies, The Owl and the Pussy-cat, by Edward Lear. The Ning Nang Nong, by Spike Milligan.

For Older Children: Stephen Fry: The Ode Less Travelled 2005, (Random House) – For those who wish to find out more on the technicalities of writing poetry.

About Me

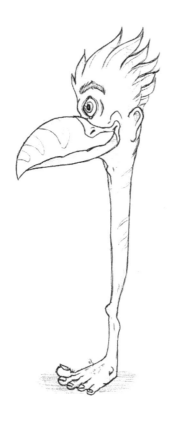

Michael Skyner has dyslexia amongst other things. He is a big kid in a bigger body. He got this from his father – he never grew up either. When he's not writing poetry, he writes zany comic fantasy for children and adults. He lives and works in Nottinghamshire.

More from *funreads*

Human sacrifice, sea monsters, starvation, cruelty and cannibals await the crew of the Sinka Maria, as the fearless explorer, Chris Clotbo sets sail for the Americas, in search of fame, fortune and the fabled gold of El Dorado. Will Clotbo succeed or will he be outsmarted by the Utilxles; the native population, and fall victim to Botella - evil servant of the Spanish Inquisition.
Chris Clotbo and the Conquest of the Americas will appeal to children who enjoy adventurous and wacky tales, daft characters and plots, with gory bits and a little bit of history thrown in for good measure.

ISBN:978-1-78610-646-9
Available from: Amazon, Barns and Noble, Feed a Read.

https://www.amazon.co.uk/-Michael-Skyner/dp/1786106469
https://www.facebook.com/Michael-Skyner-288238417951786/
https://www.feedaread.com

More from *funreads*

The Spooky Tales of Blatherington Hall

Lady Petunia Hooter shot into the room like a rocket on boosters. With the arrival of the Hooters, the peaceful co-existence of the inhabitants of Blatherington Hall comes to an end. Faced with the complete annihilation of their way of life or should that be death? The residents of the Hall are given no choice – the Hooters will have to go. And thus, the battle for Blatherington Hall begins…
For ages nine and upwards.

ISBN 978-1-78610-646-9

Available from: Amazon, Barns and Noble, Feed a Read.

https://www.amazon.co.uk/dp/B08DD774LK
https://www.facebook.com/Michael-Skyner-288238417951786/
https://www.feedaread.com

Acknowledgments

My thanks to Feedaread, Deborah and Peikwan my
proofreaders, Chandler's Book Design,
Samuel, Jonathan and Tom, my child readers,
Jenny, and the writing group; Nicola Jayne, for the fantastic
drawings and my long-suffering partner, Mariana.

With a special thank you to Dyslexia Action without
which this book would not have been possible.

If I can encourage more children to find fun in reading and if just one child overcomes their barriers to reading through Monkey, then I truly will have Jibber Jabber Joobed.

(Silly Verse for Kids, 1959, Spike Milligan).

Just One More Thing

If you liked reading my book and have the time, I would love you to give me some feedback or review the book. Your support really does make a difference and I read all the reviews personally so I can get your feedback and make this book even better.

If you'd like to leave a review then all you need to do is click the review link on this book's page on Amazon or wherever you bought the book.

Available from: Amazon, Barns and Noble, Feed a Read.

https://www.amazon.co.uk/dp/B08BQ8NTLJ
https://www.facebook.com/Michael-Skyner-288238417951786/
https://www.feedaread.com

funreads at www.mikeskyner.co.uk/